Josey Johnson's Hair and the Holy Spirit

Esau McCaulley

ILLUSTRATED BY

LaTonya Jackson

IVP Kids

TO MY TWO DAUGHTERS, CLARE AND MIRIAM:

God made you Black and beautiful.
I hope this book reminds you of his
goodness and the glorious creativity
he displayed in making you.

—Esau

FOR MY SON, ANTOIN K.:

God counted every
strand of hair on your head;
every bit of you is made
with love and purpose.

—LaTonya

InterVarsity Press • P.O. Box 1400, Downers Grove, IL 60515-1426
ivpress.com • email@ivpress.com

Text ©2022 by Esau McCaulley
Illustrations ©2022 by InterVarsity Press, LLC

InterVarsity Press® is the book-publishing division of InterVarsity Christian Fellowship/USA®,
a movement of students and faculty active on campus at hundreds of universities, colleges, and schools
of nursing in the United States of America, and a member movement of the International Fellowship
of Evangelical Students. For information about local and regional activities, visit intervarsity.org.

Cover and interior illustrations: LaTonya Jackson

ISBN 978-1-5140-0357-2 (print) • ISBN 978-1-5140-0358-9 (digital) • ISBN 978-1-5140-0548-4 (enhanced digital)

Printed in China

Library of Congress Cataloging-in-Publication Data

A catalog record for this book is available from the Library of Congress.

P 20 19 18 17 16 15 14 13 12 11 10 9 8 7 6 5 4 3 2 1

Y 38 37 36 35 34 33 32 31 30 29 28 27 26 25 24 23 22

Josey Johnson's hair
is a wonderful adventure—
it's different all the time!

SUNDAY   MONDAY   TUESDAY   WEDNE

Some days it's

a ponytail

or pigtails

or a curly afro.

And some days Josey's hair has a mind of its own!

Josey's church is celebrating something called Pentecost.

Josey does not know much about Pentecost— but she does know that she is having her hair braided, and that she needs a **new red dress!**

On Saturday Josey woke up early.

**She couldn't wait for
a day out with Dad!**

After a bowl of cereal for Josey and
a cup of coffee for Dad, it was
time to go to Monique's.

She was so excited that she
ignored the imaginary
freeze rays from
her little brother,

the karate chop from her little sister,

and even the way her big brother ignored her.

Monique's hair salon is a cute little pink building right across the street from All Nations Church.

All Nations is where Josey and her family worship on Sundays.

Monique sings in the choir at All Nations.

She also sings while she twists and braids hair. Everyone says that she has the best voice in the city!

At Josey's school, most of the girls have straight hair.
It's the same when she watches cartoons and movies.
Some days Josey feels different,

and different can be hard.

As they waited for Josey's turn in Monique's salon chair, Dad nudged her. "What are you thinking about?"

"My hair. I'm thinking about how **my hair isn't like a lot of other girls' hair.**"

Just then, Monique called Josey's name and took her to the big sink to wash and condition her hair.

Josey loved the warm wind of the blow dryer.

Once Josey's hair was dry, Monique started working oil through it, combing it, and dividing it into sections.

As Monique started the work of weaving braid after braid, Dad pulled a chair over so he and Josey could continue their conversation.

"Josey, when God created the world, was there just one kind of fish or thousands?" he asked.

"Thousands," said Josey.

"And when it was time to create the flowers, did God make them all red? Or all the same shape?" Dad continued.

"God made them every color and shape!"

Josey thought for a moment.
"I guess it's the same for people.
We're all different colors and shapes."

"But Dad," Josey paused,
"why did God make us different?"

Dad smiled, "We're all different because God is creative. Each one of us is God's unique work of art."

Dad continued,
"The Bible says
that we are 'fearfully and wonderfully made.'"

"Fearfully made?
Does that mean that we're scary?" Josey wondered.

Dad grinned. "It means you are special and worthy of honor. All of us are!"

"Josey, your Black hair,
Black lips, and Black skin are
God's work of art!"

Josey giggled. "But I'm glad I don't have to be stuck in **a museum!**"

Monique had been humming quietly as she braided Josey's hair. But right then she started singing louder.

Two stylists joined in, and then Josey started singing too because "Melodies From Heaven" is her very favorite gospel song.

As Dad's deep voice sang,
"Fill me with your precious
Holy Ghost," his eyes shone bright.

The song finished but
Monique kept humming
as she finished her work.

When Josey's hair was braided,
Monique handed Josey a mirror so
she could see the back of her head.
"What do you think?"

"I love it! Thank you, Monique."

Monique smiled
and replied,
"Off you go now.
Other beautiful
girls are waiting
their turn."

Next, Josey and Dad headed
out to find a dress.
As they looked around,
Josey asked,

"What is Pentecost?"

"After Jesus rose from
the dead, he told all his
disciples to wait in Jerusalem for
the gift of the Holy Spirit. So they
all got together to pray and to wait."

"How long did they wait?"

Josey wondered.

"Fifty days! Then the Holy Spirit appeared as small flames above their heads—what the Bible calls 'tongues of fire,'" Dad replied.

Josey imagined a small fire over her own head.

"Were they burned?"

"They weren't! But the fire gave them the power to speak in different languages. Then they began to tell other people all that God had done."

Dad smiled. "Josey, Jesus' life, death, and resurrection is for **all people,** no matter what language they speak, the color of their skin, or the curl of their hair. That's what we celebrate on Pentecost!"

"And red is for the flames of the Holy Spirit!" exclaimed Josey.

The next morning
at church, Josey looked
around and realized that her
church was like Pentecost—
it had all different kinds
of people. And it was
all so beautiful!

As everyone stood and began to sing,
Josey looked up at her dad and whispered,
"Happy Pentecost!"

A Note from the Author

I wrote this story about Josey Johnson for my daughters and for little Black girls everywhere. I want them to know that God created them as beautiful Black girls who bear the image of God.

But Josey's story can help *all* children appreciate the fact that even though we may look different, God values us each the same. God does not rank us based on the color of our skin or the curl of our hair. In fact, our differences—what makes us each unique—are part of God's good design.

How can we know this to be true? Because we learn in Genesis that we are all made in the image of God. We—*all* human beings—are the part of God's creation that was called *very good*! Throughout the Bible, we are reminded over and over again of how our differences bring God glory. He wants all people to be represented in his kingdom. And Pentecost celebrates God's desire to gather believers from all over the world into his family.

Sometimes children do not know how to speak about differences without making value judgments. For children, "this is *different*" can mean "this is *strange*," so it's important to affirm and celebrate our unique physical traits and personality traits as part of God's creative and intentionally diverse design. It might even be helpful to talk about the contributions of Christians from different ethnicities and cultures around the world so that children start to grow in awareness of different communities beyond their own neighborhood.

After you've read this book together, consider discussing these questions:

> *What kinds of differences do you notice in your classmates, friends, or neighbors?*
>
> *What does God think about those differences?*

My prayer for all of us is that we learn to appreciate this wonderful, beautiful, and diverse family of people that God has gathered into his church for his glory. May each child and adult who reads this book be reminded of just how much we are all loved and valued by God!

I praise you, for I am fearfully and wonderfully made.

PSALM 139:14